The Official Barbie Annual

£5.99

This Barbie™ Annual belongs to

Name: Holly...

Age: 7...

Address: 4 Ryde Drive...

....

My favourite Barbie® doll is.....Barbie.........................

Written by Caroline Brook.
Designed by Paul Brunton, Primary Design.
Published by Grandreams Limited, 435-437 Edgware Road
Little Venice, London W2 1TH.

contents

20

26

12

36

A Message from Barbie

Hello, and welcome to my new Annual!

I want to welcome you, my very special friends, to my new Annual. I hope you enjoy reading the stories and features I've collected for you.

It's been a busy year for me, and for my family and friends, too. In spring, Skipper really enjoyed the special birthday party I organized for her. A couple of weeks later we all had fun putting on a special show at the dance school my sisters go to.

In summer I spent some time at home, where we had a very colourful picnic. I enjoyed myself far away from home, too, when I went to the Hawaiian islands with Ken. You can read all about what we got up to there on page 36.

Autumn is the time when the new school year starts after the long summer break. We made it extra special this year, with a fun weekend for my special friend, Teresa.

My busy year ended with another holiday in a very special place called Silver World. Turn to page 54 to read all about it.

Have fun!

Love from your very special friend,

Perfect Paradise

Barbie's Rainbow Picnic

Silver World

Are You a Good Friend?

My Special Family

Meet my kid sister, Skipper. She just loves baby-sitting!

My little sister Stacie likes bowling. So do her friends Janet and Whitney.

Shelly is the baby of our family. She likes looking after her own baby doll.

My pets are an important part of the family, too!

9

My Special Friends

Ken is the best friend a girl could have. He has a very special place in my heart.

Teresa and I have been friends since we were little. She's the person I share my special secrets with.

Christie and I have been friends for ages. Christie is always lots of fun to have around!

Here's a photograph of another of my very special friends – YOU!

Barbie and the Bowling Party

Barbie was really pleased when she was asked to design a new range of clothes with a sporty look. She worked really hard on the designs. When she went to show them to the people who were going to make and sell them, she explained her ideas.

"Sports clothes have to look good, sure, but they also have to be practical.

"Sports clothes have to look good, sure, but they also have to be practical…"

I've chosen natural fabrics that are comfortable, and easy to look after. The clothes are specially cut so they're good to move around in, whatever sport you're playing."

The clients loved Barbie's designs.

As soon as they had some sample clothes made up, they asked Barbie to try them out.

As soon as they had some sample clothes made up, they asked

Barbie to try them out. They planned to take lots of photographs to put in glossy fashion magazines to make sure everyone saw the new designs.

They planned to take lots of photographs to put in glossy fashion magazines.

Barbie was glad to help, and she asked Christie and Teresa to help her model the new range. Barbie had an idea about the photo shoot. "Some of the clothes in the range have a bowling theme, so let's go along to the new bowling alley at the mall!" she suggested.

"Some of the clothes in the range have a bowling theme…"

Everyone liked the idea. The bowl was the perfect place.

Skipper was excited when she heard about the photo session. "Do you think I could go along to watch, Barbie?" she asked. "I loved seeing how you worked on the drawings, so I'd like to see how the clothes look now they're made up. And there's something else – I've haven't been to the new bowling alley yet!"

Barbie was happy to take Skipper to the photo shoot with her.

Barbie was happy to take Skipper to the photo shoot with her. "Maybe the stylists will let you give them a hand," she said.

Barbie's sporty clothes not only looked great, they felt great to wear, too.

Barbie's sporty clothes not only looked

great, they felt great to wear, too. They were perfect active casual wear.

Hooded dresses, cropped sweaters and flared leggings were all made in comfortable fabrics that stretched and moved as Barbie and her friends posed. Barbie had used vivid, bright colours, with patterns of stripes and dots. And she hadn't forgotten those all-important little details that make good designs into great designs, like zippers and fancy stitching.

"Well, what do you think, Skipper?" asked Barbie as she and her friends modelled the last outfits. They were wearing bowling shirts with their names spelled out across the front: BARBIE, CHRISTIE and TERESA. "Do you like the real clothes as much as you liked my drawings?"

"I love all the clothes," said Skipper. "They're great."

"I love all the clothes," said Skipper. "They're great. But I just adore those bowling shirts with your names on them. I'd love one of those!"

Skipper enjoyed her day with her big sister. She liked watching the stylists and makeup artists at work, and loved it when the photographer asked her if she'd like to help set up and take a few shots.

A great day ended with a game of bowls with Barbie and her friends.

A great day ended with a game of bowls with Barbie and her friends. It was fun rolling the ball down the lane, seeing it head for the pins, and knock them over with a clatter.

Barbie was pleased that Skipper enjoyed the day…

Barbie was pleased that Skipper enjoyed the day at the bowling alley so much. She had been wondering what to do for Skipper's birthday.

"Now I know the perfect sort of party for Skipper…"

"Now I know the perfect sort of party for Skipper," she whispered to Christie. "A bowling party!"

Barbie got busy over the next few days. It was hard to keep the bowling party a secret…

Barbie got busy over the next few days. It was hard to keep the bowling party a secret, but she made it to the morning of Skipper's birthday without her sister suspecting a thing.

Barbie took Skipper to the shops in the mall to choose a new outfit as a birthday gift. "We'll go home now," Barbie told her as the shop assistant wrapped it up.

"But I have to call at the bowl first. I want to book a game for next week."

"But I have to call at the bowl first. I want to book a game for next week." What a surprise Skipper got when she found her friends waiting for her in the bowling alley! Barbie had invited some of her own friends to the party, too.

"Surprise!" they all called out. "Happy birthday, Skipper!"

Barbie had bowling shirts for all the guests. Their names were spelled out across the front.

Barbie had bowling shirts for all the guests. Their names were spelled out across the front. There was one for Skipper, too, of course.

Skipper and her friends all had a great time. They played on two teams.

Skipper and her friends all had a great time. They played on two teams. Barbie was the captain of one team, and Skipper was the captain of the other. The bowling game

ended when they both knocked down all ten pins to score strikes with their final balls.

"It's a draw, the perfect result!" laughed Barbie. "Well played, sis!"

"It's a draw, the perfect result!" laughed Barbie. "Well played, sis!"

The surprises weren't over for Skipper. After the game Barbie took everyone to the restaurant for a meal.

The party ended on a high note when Skipper got to blow out the candles on a special cake that Barbie had made for her.

16

The party ended on a high note when Skipper got to blow out the candles on a special cake that Barbie had made for her. It was shaped like a bowling ball with a big letter S in chocolate icing!

"Wow!" said Skipper when she saw it. "That's a really neat cake."

"Wow!" said Skipper when she saw it. "That's a really neat cake. It must have been difficult to make it."

Barbie laughed as she watched Skipper blow out the candles.

Barbie laughed as she watched Skipper blow out the candles. "No, the cake was easy," she said. "The only difficult thing about this surprise party was keeping it a secret from you! Happy birthday, Skipper!"

17

Colours Colours Colours!

Imagine what a dull place the world would be without colours! They are all around you, and they can change your moods, and even the way you feel. Colours can make you feel calm or excited. They can make you feel happy or thoughtful, too.

MOOD COLOURS

WARM	CALM	FRESH	EXCITING
CREAM	AQUA	HOT ORANGE	DEEP PURPLE
GREEN	PALE BABY BLUE	YELLOW	BRIGHT RED
SOFT GREY	PALEST PINK	PINK	
SOFT BLUE			GOLD
BRICK	WHITE	LEAF GREEN	

18

Colours can change the way you look, too. Everyone is different, and some colours look better on you than others. Some suit you, and some don't. There are no rules, no 'good' or 'bad' colours, just colours that work well for you – or don't!

Try to learn which colours suit you best. Do it with a friend, so you can help each other. Hold clothes in different colours close to your face and take a long, hard look in the mirror. You'll soon see which colours look best on you.

The colours you like can show the kind of person you are. Which of these describes you best?

If you like...

Red, yellow – you are bold, confident and fun-loving

Green, grey – you are kind and thoughtful, a perfect friend

Blue, pink – you are quiet with a warm heart

Purple, orange – you are outgoing, friendly, ready to try new things

"Do you have a favourite colour? I like lots! I like pale colours, like baby blue, as well as bold colours, like orange. And bright pink has always been lucky for me!"

Barbie Gets it Together

Barbie was talking to her friend Christie on the telephone.

"What are you up to?" Christie asked.

"I've got a few things planned for tomorrow," Barbie replied. "I want to plant some seeds for summer flowers in the morning, then in the afternoon I'm going to spring clean my wardrobe."

"Clean it?" asked Christie. "Your wardrobe?"

Barbie laughed. "Not exactly," she said. "I always try to sort out all my clothes at the start of each new season. I've just bought a couple of new things for spring, and I want to add them to the clothes I already have. I like to keep things neat and tidy."

"That's great news!" said Christie. "I've just put my name down for a new course at the local college. I'm going to learn how to help people organize storage, and get the best out of their clothes. I need some tips from an expert – and that means you, Barbie! You always seem to know just what colours and styles suit you, and look perfectly put together. Can I come and help?"

Barbie laughed. "I can't refuse an offer like that, Christie!" she said. "Come over after lunch."

When Christie arrived, Barbie was making strawberry pancakes for her sisters, Skipper and Stacie. They were very interested in what Barbie and Christie were going to get up to.

"If there's anything I don't wear anymore, I swap it, give it to a friend, or take it down to the charity shop."

"Can we help, too, Barbie?" asked Skipper. "Looking through your clothes is such good fun."

"Oh, please say yes, Barbie," said Stacie. "Looking at your dresses and

things is my very favourite thing."

Barbie smiled. "OK, you two can help too," she said. "We should be finished quite quickly, with four of us all working together. Come on!"

Upstairs in her bedroom, Barbie opened the doors of her wardrobes. "Wow!" said Christie. "Everything is so neat and tidy."

Barbie had hung up all her clothes in neat rows. Dresses, tops, trousers and skirts were all grouped together, with the same colours next to each other. Her shoes and bags and scarves were set out in groups, too.

She explained what she was going to do. "At the start of each season, I look through all my things. If there's anything I don't wear anymore, I swap it, give it to a friend, or take it down to the charity shop."

"Then you fill the spaces with lots of new things, right?" said Christie.

Barbie laughed. "Wrong!" she said. "I don't buy many new things, you know. And I always make sure

21

that any new things I do buy match and mix in with things I already have. That way, I get good value out of my things. Even something small like a new scarf can make an old outfit look like a new one."

"When I wear this one new thing with older clothes, it will make them look like brand new outfits."

Barbie held up a bright red top with a pattern of butterflies, leaves and flowers across the front. "Look at this top. It will go with lots of things I already have, like white jeans and pedal pushers, and denims. When I wear this one new thing with older clothes, it will make them look like brand new outfits. You don't need to keep buying lots of new things if you make good use of the ones you already have."

"That's it!" said Barbie. "You've got it! You need far fewer new things if you make good use of all your clothes."

"I see what you mean," said Christie, looking through Barbie's clothes. "The way you hang things up together, and keep everything in its right place means nothing gets forgotten about. You can use a mix of old and new things together."

"That's it!" said Barbie. "You've got it! You need far fewer new things if you make good use of all your clothes."

Skipper and Stacie watched as Barbie and Christie sorted everything out. It didn't take long, and soon there was only one wardrobe left unopened.

"This is my favourite," Stacie whispered to Skipper.

"Mine too," said Skipper, as Barbie opened the doors.

Barbie and Teresa put on a little fashion show for the girls.

Inside hung Barbie's ball gowns, and the jewelled and embroidered costumes and dresses she wore for special evenings. There were dresses and jackets made in silky satin and shimmering silk, decorated with frothy lace and shimmering pearls, sequins and gem stones. On a shelf there were tiaras, feather boas and little evening bags covered in

beads. There were silver, gold and satin slippers to match each outfit.

"Try some on for us, Barbie!" said Stacie. "You, too, Teresa."

"Yes, I love seeing you wear your most special dresses," said Skipper.

Barbie and Teresa put on a little fashion show for the girls. They tried on lots of Barbie's prettiest dresses.

Barbie tried on a dress with a pink top and a soft skirt covered in rosebuds. "This dress always makes me feel like dancing!" she said, and she twirled around the bedroom.

"You look just like a princess," said Skipper.

Stacie nodded and clapped her hands.

"Yes – a dancing princess!"

Barbie stopped dancing, and gave Skipper and Stacie a big smile. "Dancing princesses!" she said. "Skipper, you're a genius! You, too, Stacie!"

The girls didn't understand, so their big sister explained. "You know how your dancing school puts on a show each year?" she asked.

The girls nodded.

"Well, this year no one has been able to come up with a story for the show – until now. When you said I look like a dancing princess, you made me think of a fairy story about twelve dancing princesses. It will be the perfect name for the show."

"You made me think of a fairy story about twelve dancing princesses. It will be the perfect name for the show."

"But who are the twelve dancing princesses?" asked Stacie.

"Sit on the bed, and I'll tell you the story," said Barbie. The girls didn't make a sound as they listened. When Barbie's story was finished, they agreed that it was perfect for the dance show.

When Barbie's story was finished, they agreed that it was perfect for the dance show.

Barbie, the other helpers and the young dancers all worked hard over the next few weeks.

There were costumes to make, and dances to practise. But the hard work was worth it, and the show was a big success.

The other girls did dances that told the story wearing lovely dresses that were copies of some of Barbie's favourites.

Skipper, Stacie and the other girls did dances that told the story wearing lovely dresses that were copies of some of Barbie's favourites.

At the end of the show, the audience clapped and cheered. Barbie gave her sisters a big hug. "You were

"You were just great!" she told them. "I'm very proud of you."

just great!" she told them. "I'm very proud of you. You're my very own dancing princesses!"

The Twelve Dancing Princesses

"The story of the twelve dancing princesses is one of my favourites. I hope you enjoy it."

Once, long ago, a king had twelve daughters. He was very proud of the princesses. He bought them lovely dresses, and shoes made of satin.

Every night, the king said good night to the twelve princesses.

But every morning, he found that their satin shoes were worn out. They were full of little holes!

The king could not understand it. "What have you been doing?" he asked.

The princesses yawned, and smiled. "Sleeping, of course, Father," they said.

The king said he would give a reward to anyone who could find out the princesses' secret.

The king said he would give a reward to anyone who could find out the princesses' secret.

A young man came to the castle. He had a special cloak that made him invisible.

The princesses, in their best dresses, went down a secret stairway.

26

He could see the princesses, but they could not see him.

"I do not want gold," he said. "I want to marry your daughter."

That night, he went to their room. The princesses, in their best dresses, went down a secret stairway. Twelve little boats waited for them on the river outside. Inside each one sat a prince.

The princes took the princesses to a tiny island. There they danced right through the night. No wonder their shoes were worn out!

The young man told the king about the dancing.

"Thank you," said the king. "Choose your reward. Do you want gold?"

The young man had fallen in love with the youngest princess. He shook his head.

"I do not want gold," he said. "I want to marry your daughter."

The king agreed, and the young man and the princess lived happily ever after.

Barbie's Rainbow Picnic

Barbie had been working hard, as usual! She had been chosen to present a new television series called *All Change*. People who wanted to make their gardens look good asked Barbie and her team to help them with new ideas. The work they did – and the new gardens – were shown on television.

Making the series took quite a long time. It was hard work. At the end of a busy few weeks of filming, Barbie felt very proud of the show. "Now I've earned some time off," she decided.

"I've seen a lot of other people's gardens," she told Skipper. "But not much of my own!"

When filming for the last programme was finished, Barbie headed for home.

Barbie had picked up lots of gardening tips on the show.

"I've seen a lot of other people's gardens," she told Skipper. "But not much of my own!"

Barbie had picked up lots of gardening tips on the show. She was keen to try out some ideas in her own garden, and she got to work after a relaxing weekend. She was planning her very own garden makeover.

"Great job, all of you!" said Barbie. "Many hands really do make light work!"

Barbie drew a plan of her garden, then added her new ideas. That was fun, but the best part came next: the digging and building and planting work. It didn't take too long because, as usual, Barbie's friends were all glad to help. Working together, the garden took shape very quickly. "Great job, all of you!" said Barbie. "Many hands really do make light work!"

Soon the new garden was finished. Barbie was really pleased with it. She was grateful for her friends' hard work, and wanted to thank them

in a fun way. She had the perfect idea. "I want you all to come back on Saturday," she told them. "We're going to have a big picnic. It's my way of saying an extra special thank you for all your help."

Barbie and her friends had planted long rows of cherry trees. They were already covered in pretty pink and white blossom.

"It's just the place for a picnic," Barbie decided. "And I'll use the colours of the blossom as the theme for the picnic."

"It's just the place for a picnic," Barbie decided.

"And I'll use the colours of the blossom as the theme for the picnic."

Saturday was the perfect day for a picnic. The weather was warm, and the sun shone brightly. When Barbie's friends arrived they found that Barbie had been really busy! She had laid out soft picnic blankets on the grass and covered

29

them with pink and white cloths. Pink and white bowls and plates sat on petal-shaped mats, all piled high with pink and white foods. There were pink prawn pizzas, cookies covered in white icing, and jugs of cherry pink fruit drink.

"Wow, you've worked hard, Barbie!" said her friend Teresa.

"Wow, you've worked hard, Barbie!" said her friend Teresa. "The picnic looks great." She took a sip from a pink tumbler. "Look, everyone, Barbie has even frozen whole fruits in ice cubes to keep the drinks cool!"

"Look, everyone, Barbie has even frozen whole fruits in ice cubes to keep the drinks cool!

Barbie and her friends ate under the shade of the trees. As they chatted and laughed, pretty cherry blossom petals drifted down from the branches.

"It's raining cherry petals," laughed Barbie.

Barbie's baby sister Shelly clapped her hands in delight, and ran around trying to catch as many of the petals as she could.

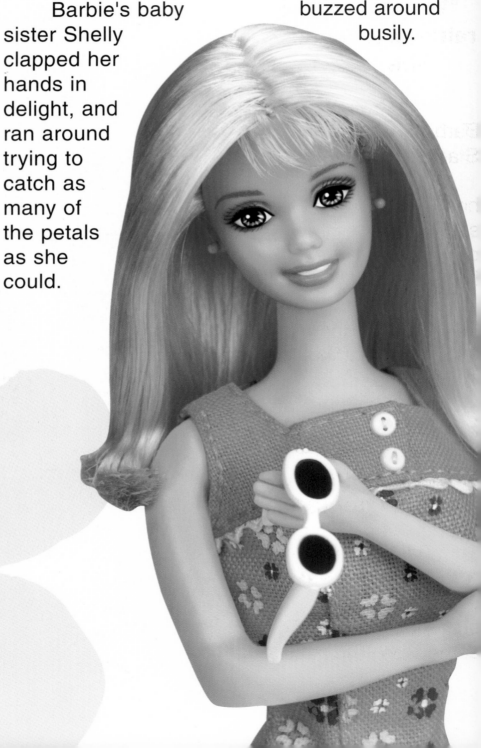

She made everyone laugh.

"It's raining cherry petals," laughed Barbie. "Showers of flowers!"

Barbie's other little sister, Stacie, watched as butterflies flitted around from flower to flower, and bees buzzed around busily.

"Look!" she shouted when a glittering dragonfly landed on Teresa's hair. Everyone watched, suddenly quiet, amazed by its shimmering rainbow colours.

Skipper looked thoughtful. "Why do we see rainbows, Barbie?" she asked.

"It's a dragonfly," Barbie whispered to Stacie.

Stacie shook her head. "No, it's not," she said. "It has more colours than a dragon. I think it's a rainbow-fly!"

Skipper looked thoughtful. "Why do we see rainbows, Barbie?" she asked.

"I want to see a rainbow," said Stacie. "I really wish I could."

Barbie explained. "We see rainbows in the sky when it is sunny and rainy at the same time. The light of the sun shines through the raindrops and splits the light into bands of colour."

"I want to see a rainbow," said Stacie. "I really wish I could."

Barbie looked up at the sky. It was clear and blue.

Barbie looked up at the sky. It was clear and blue.

31

There were no rainclouds in sight. "Sorry, Stacie, but I don't think we'll see a rainbow today," she said. "It's not the right sort of weather."

"Never mind," said Stacie, and she ran off to chase petals again.

But Barbie had an idea of how she could make Stacie's wish come true. She sneaked off with Teresa and explained what they were going to do.

"We have to uncoil the long garden hose, then I'll stand in front of the sun. When I give the signal, turn on the tap, and we'll see what happens!"

"We have to uncoil the long garden hose, then I'll stand in front of the sun.

"When I give the signal, turn on the tap, and we'll see what happens!"

When everything was ready, Barbie gave the signal, and called out, "Look, Stacie! Look, everyone!"

The petal chase ended as Stacie looked up and saw something that made her clap her hands in delight.

Barbie held the hose in the air, and sent a tall spray of water high into the air.

Stacie looked up and saw something that made her clap her hands in delight.

As she did this, the sun shone on the thousands and thousands of tiny droplets of water. They sparkled and shimmered, and coloured bands of light spread across the sky above her.

"Look, Barbie made a rainbow," said Stacie. "A lovely rainbow – just for me!"

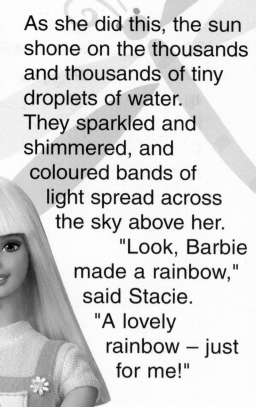

Barbie's Cherry Pink Drink

"Here's how to make the cherry pink drink and fruity ice cubes I made for the picnic."

You will need:

- 550ml milk

- 6 heaped tablespoons of cherry ice cream

- a tin of cherries in syrup

1. Ask a grown-up to open the tin of cherries. Carefully drain off the juice, but do not throw it away.

2. Now put one cherry in each cup of the ice cube tray. Make sure there are no stones in them.

3. Put a teaspoon of cherry juice in each cup. Fill the tray with water. Ask a grown-up to put the tray in the freezer.

4. When the ice cubes are frozen hard, make the drink. Put the ice cream and milk in a bowl and mix with a whisk.

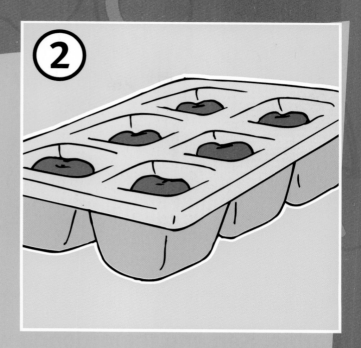

"That's it! Pour the drink
into glasses, and add
2 or 3 cherry ice cubes
to each drink. Use
strawberries instead of
cherries if you like."

Perfect Paradise

Barbie, Ken and their friends were making plans for an extra special summer holiday. It was Barbie's idea. "Let's take off for somewhere hot and tropical this year," she said when they met up to plan their holiday.

Barbie had just got back home after making her latest film. "I know the perfect place, the Hawaiian islands. That's where we shot the final scenes of the film.

"I didn't get much of a chance to explore, because I was there to work, not play."

It's magical! I didn't get much of a chance to explore, because I was there to work, not play. But I promised I'd go back one day real soon. And I'd love to show the islands to you guys. So, why don't we go together?"

"I'll fly us out to the islands in my plane," said Barbie.

"Great idea," said Ken.
"I'll fly us out to the islands in my plane," said Barbie.

"Once we get there we'll hire a sailing boat and sail around from island to island. It'll be fun helping sail with the crew, and we can stop off wherever we like."

"I can't wait!" said Barbie. "Let's plan our route right now!"

Barbie got out a map of the islands and spread it on the coffee table. "I can't wait!" said Barbie. "Let's plan our route right now!"

The holiday was even better than Barbie and her friends had hoped it would be. The seas around the islands were calm and the bright blue water stretched as far as the eye could see. Barbie and her friends got a warm welcome wherever they went.

One of the smaller islands felt extra special, so Barbie and her friends decided to stay for a while. They made friends with a young island girl, Leia. She was glad to act as their guide, and showed them the beaches where they could surf and water ski. She took them to calm bays where they could dive on the reefs that were alive with colourful tropical fish, and to white-sand beaches that were perfect for frisbee games. She took them on treks deep into the tropical forest, too.

37

"We wouldn't have seen the island animals and birds and flowers without you as our guide, Leia..."

Barbie was thrilled. "We wouldn't have seen the island animals and birds and flowers without you as our guide, Leia," she said. "You've made our stay here very special."

Later, Ken was relaxing in a hammock strung between two tall, swaying palm trees. "This is the most perfect place, Leia," he said. "You're so lucky to live here. It's paradise."

Leia forced a small smile, but Barbie noticed that she looked a little sad. "What is it?" she asked gently. "Is something wrong?"

Leia explained. "I know the island is paradise," she said.

"But looking after people on holiday is our only real way of making a living. Even so, there isn't much money, and some of the young people feel they have to leave the island to find work. It's sad, because though some of them come back, as I have, lots leave for good. We could let more tourists visit, but too many will spoil what we have here." Leia gave a little shrug.

"But what else can we do? We can't sell our sunshine, or our warm welcome and tropical colours."

Over the next couple of days, Barbie gave the problem some serious thought.

The next time she saw Leia she had lots of ideas to talk about with her.

The next time she saw Leia she had lots of ideas to talk about with her. "I know you said you couldn't sell what you have here," said Barbie. "But I'm not so sure."

"The necklaces of flowers you give to visitors as a way of saying hello are a great design theme."

"What do you mean?" asked Leia.

Barbie explained. "The necklaces of flowers you give to visitors as a way of saying hello are a great design theme. You could make them using fake flowers. The same flower designs on jewellery and hair bands and clips will look great."

Barbie pointed to Leia's sarong, a piece of soft fabric decorated with bold tropical flowers that she wore tied loosely around

"But how do we get started on something like that? We don't know anything about fashion and designing clothes and things."

her waist. "The flower patterns are wonderful for beach wear. I love them, and I just know people all over the world will want to wear them!"

"It's a great idea, Barbie," said Leia. "But how do we get started on something like that? We don't know anything about fashion

and designing clothes and things."

"You don't," said Barbie. "But I do! And I'll be glad to help you." She turned to Ken. "We all will, won't we?"

Soon she had files of designs based on the ideas she and Leia had talked about.

Back home after the holiday, Barbie got busy. Soon she had files of designs based on the ideas she and Leia had talked about. There were sarongs and bikinis in the vivid colours that could be seen all over the islands, bold blues, citrus greens and hot pinks. Some were patterned with flowers, dolphins and shells. Everyone loved the hair decorations and, of course, the necklaces of flowers.

Barbie's friends in the fashion business all loved the look.

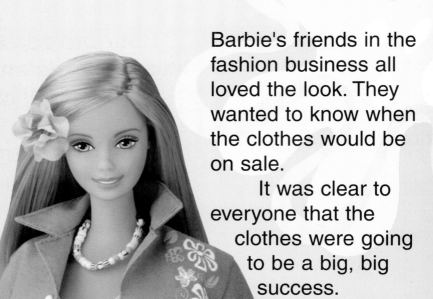

Barbie's friends in the fashion business all loved the look. They wanted to know when the clothes would be on sale.

It was clear to everyone that the clothes were going to be a big, big success.

"There's just one more thing we have to do," said Ken.

"What's that?" asked Barbie. "What have we forgotten?"

"We need to give the whole range of clothes a name," said Ken.

"Perfect!" said Barbie. "Hey, that's it. We'll call the clothes the Perfect Paradise range!"

"Mmm," said Barbie, "you're right. Any ideas?"

"Just one," said Ken. "How about Paradise?"

"Perfect!" said Barbie. "Hey, that's it. We'll call the clothes the Perfect Paradise range!"

The Perfect Paradise clothes were a big hit, and Leia and

"I want to come back to the islands soon to work on some new designs," said Barbie.

the islanders were very pleased, and grateful for Barbie's help. "We can't thank you enough," said Leia when Barbie flew her in to see the launch of the clothes at a big fashion show. "We just couldn't do it without you."

Barbie laughed. "You don't have to," she said. "I'll help all I can, on one condition."

"Name it," said Leia.

"I want to come back to the islands soon to work on some new designs," said Barbie. "It's the best excuse I know for coming back to see you on Perfect Paradise!"

All About Barbie

Try these questions to find out how much you know about Barbie. The answers are on page 60.

1. Ken wakes Barbie with a kiss. What is the name of the fairy story?

2. Skipper and her friends love yo-yos. Do you know the names of her two friends?

3. What is the name of Barbie's new four-legged friend?

4. Here's one of Barbie's oldest friends. They've known each other since they were five years old! What is her name?

Question 1.

Question 2.

Question 3.

Question 4.

43

Friends

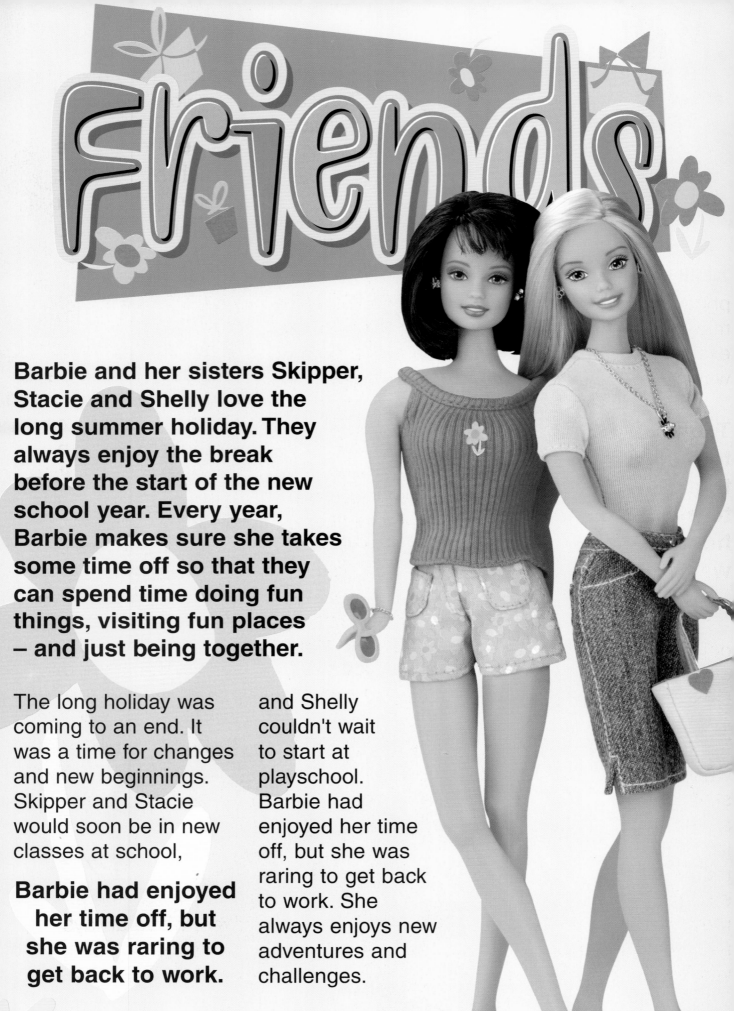

Barbie and her sisters Skipper, Stacie and Shelly love the long summer holiday. They always enjoy the break before the start of the new school year. Every year, Barbie makes sure she takes some time off so that they can spend time doing fun things, visiting fun places – and just being together.

The long holiday was coming to an end. It was a time for changes and new beginnings. Skipper and Stacie would soon be in new classes at school, and Shelly couldn't wait to start at playschool. Barbie had enjoyed her time off, but she was raring to get back to work. She always enjoys new adventures and challenges.

Barbie had enjoyed her time off, but she was raring to get back to work.

She had been asked to take some photographs for a new magazine, and she felt excited about that. She was raring to go!

Teresa was going to start a new job that meant she had to move to a new home a long way away.

There were going to be changes for Barbie's very special friend, too. Teresa was going to start a new job that meant she had to move to a new home a long way away. "It's a great job, and I'm glad to be going," Teresa told Barbie. "But I feel a little bit sad, too."

"We've shared secrets and clothes and walked to school together every day since we were five years old…"

"Why's that?" asked Barbie.

"Well, we've shared secrets and clothes and walked to school together every day since we were five years old, haven't we? I'm really going to miss you."

"The move is really exciting, and your new job is a great chance for you."

"I'm going to miss you, too," said Barbie, who shared a little bit of her special friend's sadness. "But we've both got to think positive, and look on the bright side. The move is really exciting, and your new job is a great chance for you. We'll still see lots of each other, I promise. I'll fly up to see you for weekends whenever I can. And hey, there's always the telephone!"

"We'll still see lots of each other, I promise. I'll fly up to see you for weekends whenever I can."

Teresa laughed. "Yes, we've always spent a lot of time chatting on the phone, haven't we? That doesn't have to change just because I'm moving away."

Barbie decided to make their last weekend together an extra special one. "We're going to have a Special Friends Weekend!"

Barbie decided to make their last weekend together an extra special one. "We're going to have a Special Friends Weekend!" she told Teresa. "Saturday will be just for the two of us. We'll go to the gym, have a facial and a manicure, then do some serious shopping. We'll have a pizza pyjama party in the evening, and you can sleep over.

"We'll have a pizza pyjama party in the evening, and you can sleep over."

The others all want to come over on Sunday to say goodbye, too. I've called a meeting of the Barbie Fun Club. Ken and the others are all coming over. We'll have lunch, then play tennis all afternoon. How does that sound?" Teresa was delighted. "It sounds great," she said. "I can't wait!"

After a busy week packing up her things, Teresa was ready for some fun.

After a busy week packing up her things, Teresa was ready for some fun.

After a trip to the gym and the beauty shop, the two friends had a great time buying warm clothes for Teresa. She was moving north, and was going to need them.
Back at Barbie's house she showed Skipper the chunky fairisle sweater,

duffle coat, duffle bag and quilted purse she had bought while Barbie got busy in the kitchen making pizzas.

Back at Barbie's house she showed Skipper the chunky fairisle sweater, duffle coat, duffle bag and quilted purse she had bought…

Later, after watching a movie, they piled on to Barbie's king-size bed to share hot chocolate drinks.

"Let's empty out our bags and share our special things one more time," said Teresa. "It's something I've always enjoyed, since we were kids."

Later, after watching a movie, they piled on to Barbie's king-size bed to share hot chocolate drinks.

Teresa shook out photographs, beads, and lots of other special things from her bag. She and Barbie looked at them together, and talked about the good times they had shared. They would always be happy memories.

She and Barbie looked at them together, and talked about the good times they had shared.

Teresa twisted the friendship ring on her finger. Barbie had bought it for her birthday. "I'll wear the ring every day," she said. "Every time I see and feel it, it will make me think of you."

Teresa twisted the friendship ring on her finger.

Late that night, after lots more gossip, laughs, hugs – and a few secrets – it was time for bed.

Barbie made Sunday a fun-filled day for Teresa…

47

Barbie made Sunday a fun-filled day for Teresa and their friends.

There was a big barbecue for lunch, with hot dogs and burgers, then lots of tennis.

There was a barbecue for lunch, with hot dogs and burgers, then lots of tennis.

Barbie and Teresa played as a team in the doubles, and were pleased to win the final. But Barbie had prizes for everyone, whether they had won or lost.

Barbie and Teresa played as a team in the doubles, and were pleased to win the final.

Teresa's prize was the last one Barbie gave out.

Teresa found a heart-shaped locket inside. It was exactly like the one Barbie always wore.

When she opened her little black velvet box, Teresa found a heart-shaped locket inside. It was exactly like the one Barbie always wore.

"What can I say, Barbie?" said Teresa. "It's wonderful. You're the best. Thank you."

The two friends shared a big, big hug. "We'll always be special friends…"

The two friends shared a big, big hug. "We'll always be special friends, won't we, Barbie?" said Teresa. "Wherever we are."

"You bet we will," said Barbie. "Special friends – forever."

49

Favourite Friends

"Teresa is my Special Friend. Make this frame for a picture of your Special Friend. I'll show you how, but always ask a grown-up to help you."

You will need:

- **a piece of card 20cm x 20cm**

- **safety scissors**

- **a pencil**

- **non-toxic craft glue**

- **a photograph of your Special Friend**

- **felt-tip pens**

- **a sticky tab**

1. Fold the card in half, from left to right.

2. Draw a heart on the front of the card. Now cut along the lines; copy the diagram opposite.

3. Next, place the photograph inside the card to see how it fits. You may need to trim the card.

4. Put some glue on the back of the photograph and stick it inside the card.

5. Write 'My Special Friend' on the front of the card. Decorate it with patterns.

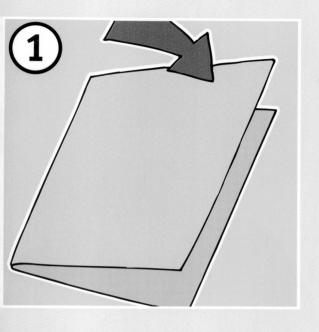

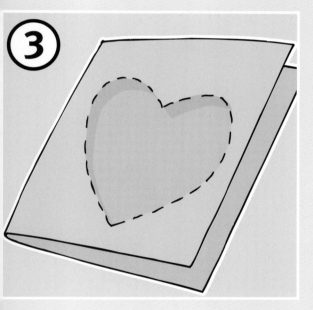

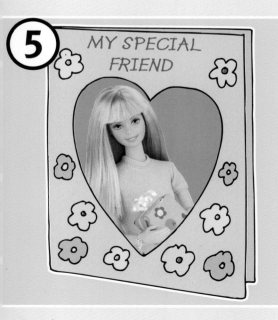

"Use a grab tab to stick the heart frame on your bedroom wall."

MY SPECIAL FRIEND

51

Are You a Good Friend?

Barbie is the best friend any girl could have. Answer these questions to find out how good a friend you are.

The answers are on page 60.

1. Your friend buys a new top that does not suit her. When she asks if you like it, do you:

a. tell her it looks brilliant
b. say it looks awful
c. suggest ways she could wear it with other things?

2. Your friend is feeling fed up. When she says she can't be bothered to go out, do you:

a. give her a big hug and say, "Let's talk about it"
b. tell her you feel fed up, too
c. go out on your own?

3. Your friend wants to join your band, but she just can't sing! Do you:

a. let her join anyway
b. tell her she sings like a frog
c. suggest she helps with the clothes and lighting?

4. Your friend likes a boy, but you hear him say unkind things about her. Do you:

a. tell her exactly what he said about her
b. suggest that perhaps he isn't right for her
c. let her go on thinking he likes her?

5. Your friend has some bad school results. She worries that she's a failure. Do you:

a. agree with her
b. tell her to think positive: "You can be anything!"
c. shrug your shoulders?

Silver World

Barbie loves to get away for a break with her friends in the winter. She often flies off somewhere warm and sunny, but last year she decided to try something different. One evening, she and Ken were sitting on the floor surrounded by glossy holiday brochures.

They were all filled with pictures of blue seas fringed by white sand beaches and swaying palm trees.

"I don't think we can top the summer holiday we had in the Hawaiian islands," said Barbie. "So let's try something different."

Ken and Barbie jumped in Barbie's new sports car and headed for the travel shop. The assistant there found just the thing for them. "It's a brand-new themed holiday centre," she told them. "It's opening this week.

54

The assistant there found just the thing for them. "It's a brand-new themed holiday centre," she told them.

It's called Silver World, and its theme is the snow-covered lands of the Arctic and Antarctic. It sounds like a really magical place. What do you think?"

"What a brilliant idea!" said Barbie. "I love it. It's just what we're looking for – somewhere really different!"

"It sounds like a really magical place. What do you think?"

Barbie's friend Christie was just

as keen. "It sounds fantastic," she said. "Let's go!"

Barbie's friend Christie was just as keen. "It sounds fantastic," she said.

Barbie, Ken and Christie didn't have long to wait for their holiday. They spent some of the time before they set off packing their winter sports gear. They were planning to do lots of skating, skiing, tobogganing and snowboarding.

They were planning to do lots of skating, skiing, tobogganing and snowboarding.

The time passed extra quickly for Barbie. She had a lot of fun designing a new range of outfits for them to wear. She got her ideas from the snow and ice colours of Silver World, and used lots of white, silver, palest pink and blue colours, all cool, icy and shimmery. She showed the glint and glisten of ice and snowflakes in tinsel fur, sparkle trims and shiny soft velvets.

Barbie's clothes weren't just about style and design. She knew that they had to work hard, too.

But Barbie's clothes weren't just about style and design. She knew that they had to work hard, too. How the clothes felt and moved was even more important than how they looked.

Barbie even added sunglasses that were the perfect combination of style and protection from the glare of the winter sun.

They had to be comfortable, warm,

and tough. Barbie even added sunglasses that were the perfect combination of style and protection from the glare of the winter sun.

Silver World really was the magical place Barbie had hoped for. Soft,

shimmering snow and glinting ice lay like a white carpet as far as they could see. Even the hotel they stayed in had frosted walls and towers.

"It's like a fairytale castle," said Christie.

"Like something out of the story of the Snow Queen!"

Barbie, Ken and Christie really enjoyed themselves. They did lots of skating, skiing and snowboarding. There were Arctic and Antarctic animals to meet, too. Barbie loved the families of penguins and got a real buzz out of helping to feed them. They got through buckets and buckets full of fish!

There were Arctic and Antarctic animals to meet, too.

Ken, Barbie and Christie had a lot of fun trying to build an igloo, a little round house made from blocks of frozen snow. It was much more difficult than it looked! Ken worked from the inside as the igloo took shape, and Barbie and Christie had to laugh when they sealed off the entrance hole with the last block of snow – with Ken inside!

Barbie and Christie had to laugh when they sealed off the entrance hole with the last block of snow – with Ken inside!

Ken thought the best day of the whole stay was when a guide took them out riding across the ice flats on skidoos. It was a real thrill to be able to watch a family of polar bears on the ice – from a safe distance, of course.

The holiday at Silver World was a very special one, but Christmas was drawing near, and Barbie found

57

her thoughts moving towards home and her family.

"Silver World is such a great place, isn't it?" she told Ken.

"Silver World is such a great place, isn't it?" she told Ken. "But Christmas is a family time, too. I'll be sorry to leave in one way, but glad to be going home in another."

Ken decided to make the last night of their stay extra special. Without telling Barbie and Christie, he organized a midnight ride in an

Without telling Barbie and Christie, he organized a midnight ride in an old-fashioned open sleigh…

old-fashioned open sleigh pulled by reindeer. The sky was a deep, velvety black, lit up only by twinkling, pinpoint stars and the lighted torches that leapt and

flamed on each side of the driver.

"What do you think?" asked Ken.

"Magical!" said Christie.

Barbie nodded in agreement. "This is the perfect end to a perfect holiday in a perfect place!"

It was late when Barbie got home. Skipper, Stacie and Shelly were fast asleep, so she didn't wake them. But the girls somehow knew that their big sister was home, and they all woke up extra early, when it was still dark outside. All three of them jumped on to her bed next morning.

"We can't wait to hear all about Silver World!" said Skipper.

"We want to hear all about it – everything!" said Stacie.

Telling them all about the holiday took quite a while, but the girls wouldn't let Barbie get up until she had told them every last detail.

"I'd love to go there one day," said Skipper.

"Me too," said Stacie. "Will you take us, Barbie?"

Shelly smiled her biggest smile. "Please?"

Barbie laughed. "I'll think about it," she said. "But not if you don't let me get up. Will you open the curtains, please, Skipper?"

Thank you, Barbie. You brought Silver World back home with you!"

Skipper pulled back the curtains and gasped. "Look!" she said, pointing into the garden, which was covered in a soft white blanket of snow. "It's snowing! Great! Thank you, Barbie. You brought Silver World back home with you!"

Answers

All About Barbie

Are You a Good Friend?

(page 42)
1 Sleeping Beauty
2 Nikki and Courtney
3 Daisy
4 Teresa

(page 52)
Score 5 points for each correct answer.
1 c
2 a
3 c
4 b
5 b

If you scored up to:
25 you are a perfect friend

20 you are a very good friend

15 you are a good friend – sometimes

10 try to be more caring

5 oh, dear!

Wish upon a Star

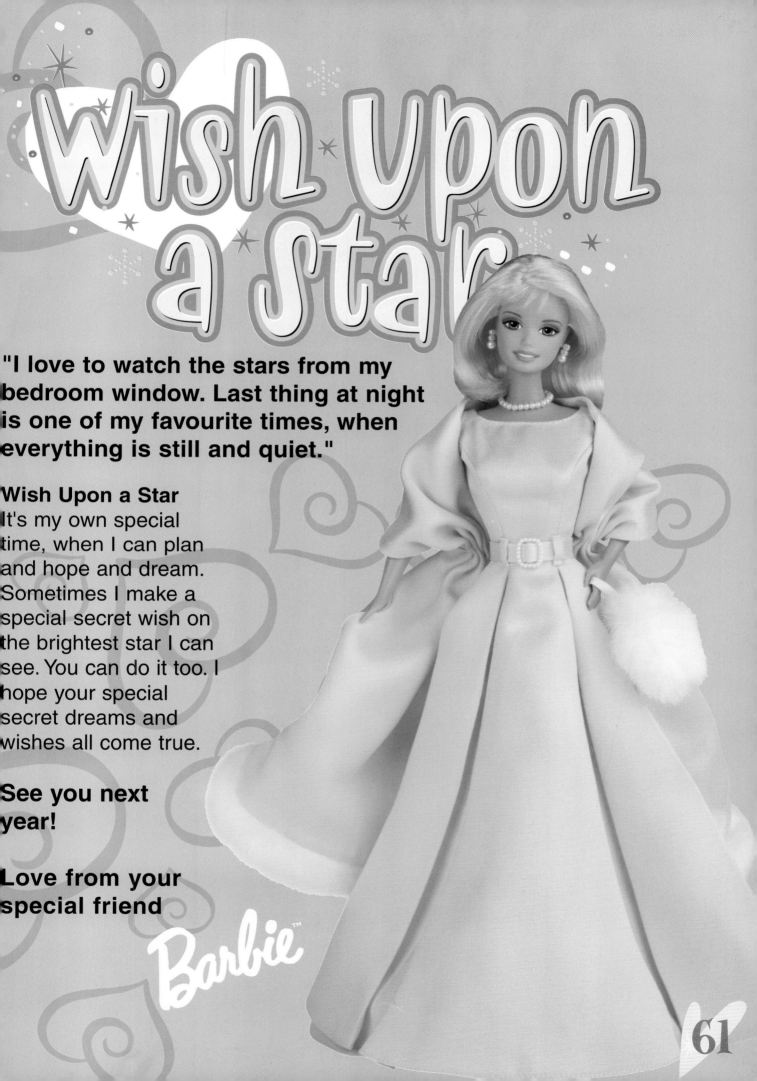

"I love to watch the stars from my bedroom window. Last thing at night is one of my favourite times, when everything is still and quiet."

Wish Upon a Star
It's my own special time, when I can plan and hope and dream. Sometimes I make a special secret wish on the brightest star I can see. You can do it too. I hope your special secret dreams and wishes all come true.

See you next year!

Love from your special friend

Barbie™